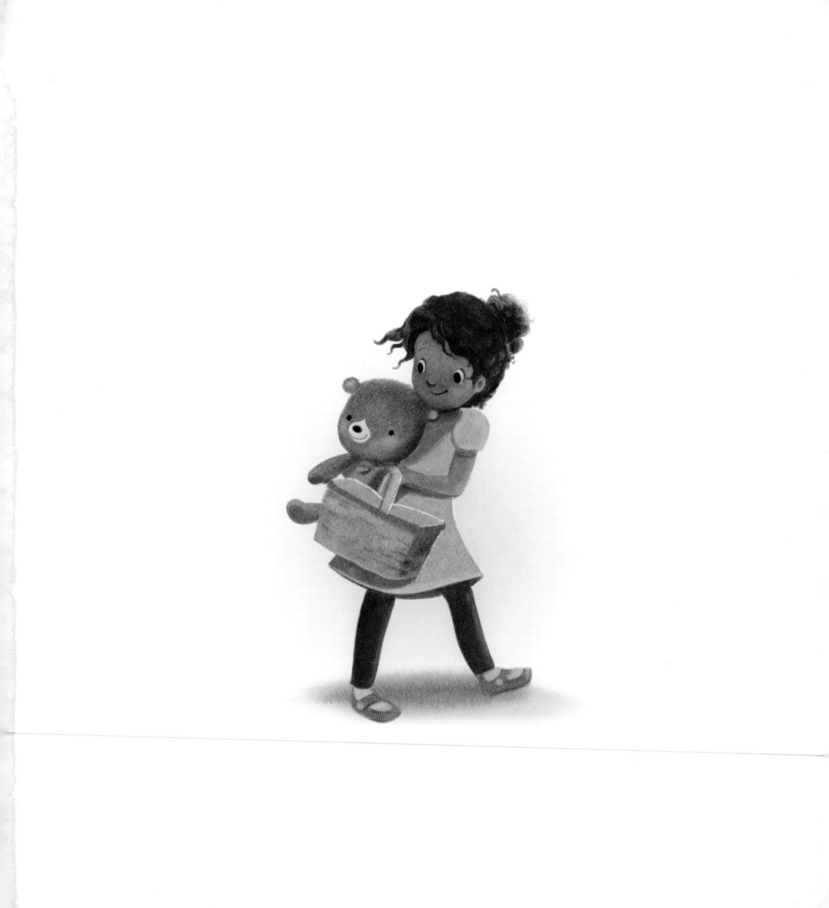

For Boo Bear, aka Samantha Swenson — VV

For my favorite teddy bear, Josh — SH

Text copyright © 2020 by Vikki VanSickle
Illustrations copyright © 2020 by Sydney Hanson

Tundra Books, an imprint of Penguin Random House Canada Young Readers,
a Penguin Random House Company

Library and Archives Canada Cataloguing in Publication

Title: Teddy bear of the year / by Vikki VanSickle ; illustrated by Sydney Hanson
Names: VanSickle, Vikki, 1982- author. | Hanson, Sydney, illustrator.
Identifiers: Canadiana (print) 20190145617 | Canadiana (ebook) 20190145625 |
ISBN 9780735263925 (hardcover) | ISBN 9780735263932 (EPUB)

Classification: LCC PS8643.A59 T43 2020 | DDC jC813/.6—dc23

Published simultaneously in the United States of America by Tundra Books of Northern New York,
an imprint of Penguin Random House Canada Young Readers, a Penguin Random House Company

Library of Congress Control Number: 2019944688

Edited by Samantha Swenson
Designed by John Martz
The artwork in this book was created with colored pencils and finished digitally.
The text was set in Aeris B Pro.

Printed and bound in China

www.penguinrandomhouse.ca

1 2 3 4 5   24 23 22 21 20

Penguin
Random House
TUNDRA BOOKS

tundra

TEDDY BEAR
OF THE YEAR

VIKKI VANSICKLE

ILLUSTRATED BY SYDNEY HANSON

tundra

Ollie thought being a teddy bear was the best job in the world. His shift started weekdays at three in the afternoon, when his girl, Amena, got home from school, and ended after breakfast the next morning. On weekends and in the summer he was on call twenty-four hours a day.

The best part of Ollie's day was the moment when Amena would burst through the door, give him a hug and tell him about her adventures.

At night, when he snuggled in next to Amena, he would think about her stories and smile.

One night, in the middle of Ollie's shift,
a shining silver sailboat appeared outside
Amena's window.

At the helm was a grizzled old teddy bear.

"Ahoy there, little buddy!" he said. "You must be Ollie. My name is Snuggles, but you can call me The Snug. I'm here to take you to the Teddy Bears' Picnic."

"The Teddy Bears' Picnic?" Ollie asked. "What's that?"

"Every summer the local chapter of the Teddy Bears' Association gets together to celebrate the year in teddy-care. As one of the longest-standing members, it's my job to pick up the first-timers — like you! Now hop in, little buddy, or there won't be any honey tarts left!"

Ollie looked at the sleeping Amena. "But, Amena —"

"Don't worry about your girl," said The Snug.
"She'll remain exactly as she is until we return.
It's Teddy Bear Magic!"

Ollie gave Amena one more cuddle before he
stepped into the silver sailboat.

"I see you know your ABCs,"
The Snug said.

Ollie was confused. "ABCs?"
he asked.

"ABCs: Always Be Cuddling.
Teddy bear 101."

The Teddy Bears' Picnic was
held deep in the woods.

When they arrived, Ollie saw teddies
of all shapes and sizes.

The Snug introduced Ollie to some of his friends from the Teddy
Bears' Association: Scottie, from the Department of Bedtime
Planning; Mr. Pants, Chief Cuddling Officer; and Jessica, Regional
Stuffing Manager and Stitchery Inspector.

They ate delicious treats,

competed in three-legged races,

and Ollie even worked up the
courage to sing bearaoke.

After Scottie's rousing rendition of "Nine to Five," a tiny pink bear took the stage and tapped the microphone.

"Is this thing on? Good evening, teddies! I'm Pinkie, and as president of the Teddy Bears' Association, I'd like to welcome everyone to this year's picnic! Tonight we recognize our members who have demonstrated excellence in teddy-care."

"First I'd like to call up Boo Bear." Pinkie pinned a star on a teddy with a curly coat. "Boo Bear sat by her boy's side through a long sickness. Without her, young Wei would have been lonely and afraid in a strange hospital bed."

Ollie was impressed — Boo Bear was so noble! Sick children need all the love and comfort a teddy can give.

"Next we have Fang." Pinkie pinned another star on a strange-looking bear with long, soft ears. "Just this past week, Fang accompanied his girl, Tina, on her first sleepover party."

Ollie clapped loudly. A sleepover! He'd never even left the yard. Fang was very brave.

"And now, a bear who needs no introduction. Snuggles — or should I say, The Snug — has been a wonderful teddy for many years, a beloved companion to not just one child, but a family of six. He has made it through the washing machine, spent a week in a crowded lost-and-found box and even survived a teddy-napping by the neighbor's dog."

The Snug moved his kerchief aside. "But not without some scars," he said.

The crowd cheered for The Snug's amazing adventures. Ollie cheered the loudest.

One by one, Pinkie pinned stars on all the deserving teddies. As she listed their achievements, Ollie felt smaller and smaller. He tried to think of a single thing that he had done that deserved a star, but nothing came to mind. He was just an ordinary bear.

"And now for our last star of the evening. The Teddy Bear of the Year Award goes to . . . Ollie!"

Ollie gasped. "Me?"

Every teddy bear at the picnic turned to smile at him.

"But — I'm just a regular bear with a regular job; I haven't done anything noble or brave or adventurous like these other teddies. I haven't done anything special at all!"

"I wouldn't be so sure about that," said Pinkie.
"Let's take a look at the events of May sixth."

Ollie's heart ached for his girl as he watched
the events unfold on the screen.

"Poor Amena. She had such
a bad day."

"Yes," Pinkie agreed.
"But wait — it isn't
over yet."

"The Teddy Bear of the Year Award is given to a young teddy who excels at the ABCs of teddy-care."

"Always Be Cuddling," Ollie said. "Teddy bear 101."

"Exactly. You turned Amena's bad day into a good day, and that is VERY special. Even the smallest actions — a cuddle, a kind word, a hug — have great impact. All of you are here tonight because you provide the comfort your children need to feel strong.
That is true Teddy Bear Magic."

Pinkie pinned a shining star to Ollie's chest. "Let's hear it for Ollie, your brand-new Teddy Bear of the Year, and for all of our teddies," she said.

After the stars had been given out, it was time to celebrate!
Ollie was so happy he thought his stitches would burst!

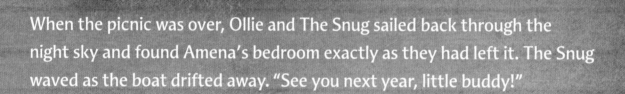

When the picnic was over, Ollie and The Snug sailed back through the night sky and found Amena's bedroom exactly as they had left it. The Snug waved as the boat drifted away. "See you next year, little buddy!"

Ollie waved good-bye before snuggling in next to Amena.

He told her all about his first great
adventure, of flying sailboats, honey tarts
and a picnic in the woods. In her sleep,
Amena smiled.